MW01015726

Order this book online at www.trafford.com
or email orders@trafford.com

Most Trafford titles are also available at major online book retailers.

Printed in Victoria, BC, Canada.

ISBN: 978-1-4269-2844-4

Library of Congress Control Number: 2010902925

*Our mission is to efficiently provide the world's finest, most comprehensive book publishing
service, enabling every author to experience success. To find out how to publish your book, your
way, and have it available worldwide, visit us online at www.trafford.com*

Trafford rev. 03/24/2010

PUBLISHING® www.trafford.com

North America & international
toll-free: 1 888 232 4444 (USA & Canada)
phone: 250 383 6864 ♦ fax: 812 355 4082

For Additional Copies
call or email
Diane Lair
250-655-3446 dianelair@shaw.ca

Miss Muggles,

The Comical Dog

Written by Diane Lair
Illustrated by Donna Jean

Diane Lair

Every Saturday afternoon, my Mom and I visit my Gramma Trudy at the Tranquility Lodge. The Tranquility Lodge is a big home for old people who can't live by themselves any more. The Lodge has doctors, nurses, cooks, and cleaning people to look after the old folks. My Gramma lives there because she doesn't walk very well, and she has a hard time cooking and cleaning and stuff like that.

Last Saturday when we went to see Gramma Trudy, our dog, Miss Muggles, (Muggles for short) came with us. Dogs are not allowed in the building (I don't know why), so we put her in the fenced-in part of the garden by the side of the Lodge. As a puppy, Muggles had been quite a brat, so we still didn't trust her very much. We knew Muggles would be safe in the garden because she couldn't get out and run away. The visiting room had huge windows over-looking the garden, so it would be easy to keep an eye on her.

When we walked into the big visiting room, all the old people were there waiting for their visitors. I looked at old Mr. Lawson sitting by the window in his wheelchair. I felt sad for him, just like I did every Saturday. He had a sort of sad, sort of grumpy face; a face that seemed unhappy all the time. I had never seen Mr. Lawson smile, never once. When I looked around the room, I realized most of the old people didn't smile much. Some of them looked sleepy. Some of them seemed bored, others lonely, but no one seemed very happy. No one was smiling, except Gramma Trudy who had spotted us as we walked into the room.

We sat beside the windows, not too far from Mr. Lawson. Gramma Trudy was asking my Mom all sorts of questions about boring stuff, so I sat and looked out the windows.

Muggles was sniffing some bushes under the windows when she glanced up and saw me. She jerked her head up and yelped at me. I smiled because I knew she wanted me to come out and play. When you have a dog, you soon understand the meaning of their barks, their yips, and all their sounds.

Muggles couldn't believe I was sitting **inside** while she was stuck **outside** all by herself. She stared at me, waited a few seconds, and then delivered several loud barks.

"Arf! Arf"! Get out here, Dummy! was her message. Of course, there was nothing I could do, so I just smiled and sat there watching her.

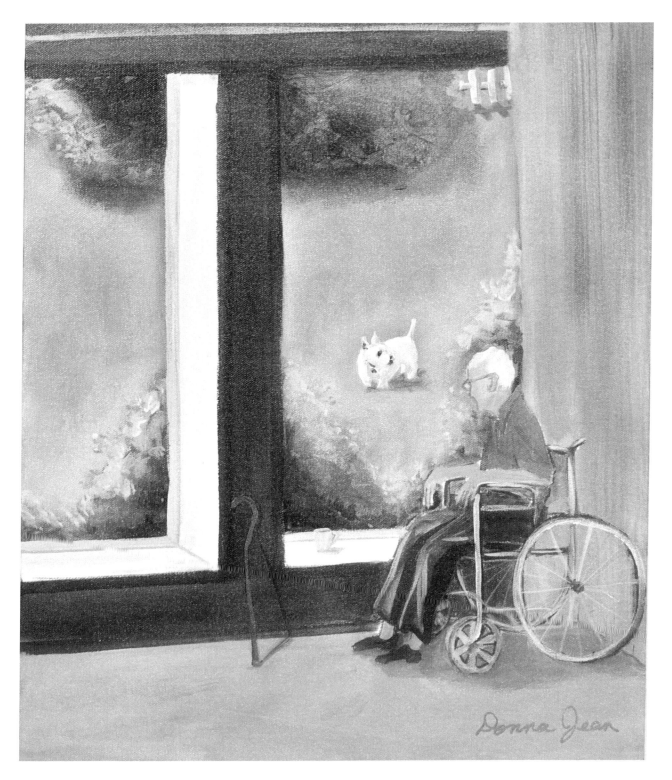

Since I hadn't responded to her barks, Muggles decided to try a different tactic. She started dashing about inside the little garden. She ran faster and faster, in and out of the bushes, around the trees, and back to the windows. It was as though her tail was on fire.

That was when I heard an unusual sound, a sort of snort/grunt/chuckle sound. I glanced up and was a little surprised to see Mr. Lawson watching Muggles. But even more surprising was the look on Mr. Lawson's face. He was smiling! The smile made his face look totally different; much better if you don't mind my saying so.

I glanced back at Muggles. She was now being completely silly. Muggles rolled around on the grass, tumbling over and over. Then she stayed on her back with all four legs up in the air. She squirmed and wiggled around as though her back was itchy. She waved all four paws in the air, barking and yipping, and twisting her head so she could look up at me and make sure I was still watching her.

Then I heard the snort/grunt/chuckle sound again. I was sure of it! Mr. Lawson had chuckled. It was the kind of chuckle that came from deep in his chest and made his face look very happy. Some of the other old folks came over to see what had caused Mr. Lawson to chuckle. They stood at the big windows and watched as my little dog continued to put on quite a show.

Donna Jean

Just then, Muggles found a little wooden block in the grass where she had been flailing about on her back. She took that little block in her mouth, tossed it high in the air, and as it fell to the ground, she leapt up and snatched it back into her mouth. She immediately flung it up again, this time grabbing the little wooden block as it landed, rolling over as she hit the ground. She was moving so quickly that she looked like a fuzzy white blur.

That's when I heard an even stranger sound. I heard a big belly laugh! Mr. Lawson had laughed out loud. He threw his head back and laughed out loud again. Some of the others giggled and chuckled, but Mr. Lawson really and truly laughed out loud over and over again. Even Muggles heard him because she stopped and stared up at him tilting her head first one way and then the other as though she was trying to figure out what that strange noise was. Her 'head-tilting' really tickled Mr. Lawson's funny bone causing his laughter to get louder and louder. Soon, most of the old people and their visitors were watching the "MISS MUGGLES' PERFORMANCE" and laughing out loud along with Mr. Lawson.

Muggles sat up on her hind legs and waved her front paws at the windows begging someone to please come out and play with her. Then she dashed about once again. She rolled over, she tossed the block, she flipped, she wiggled and she barked. Miss Muggles entertained everyone the whole while we were there, until finally, it was time to say good-bye. It was time for the old people to go to their art class. It was time for the visitors to go home. We walked outside, opened the gate, put Muggles in the car and left.

The following Saturday, we went to visit Gramma Trudy as usual.
Gramma was sitting beside Mr. Lawson. Many of the other people
were standing around them. When we walked into the big room, it
seemed like everyone had been waiting for us to arrive. Mr. Lawson
rolled his chair towards us and asked us to follow him. He led Mom
and me down a long corridor with all the others following behind. He
rolled into the art room and pointed at the walls.

It was amazing, truly amazing! The walls were covered with the art work that the old people had done. All the art work was of Miss Muggles. There was a painting of Muggles running, a drawing of her rolling over, a sketch of her playing with the little block. Over there she was tilting her head. There she was on her hind legs begging. It was amazing!

I looked around the art room. The art room looked great.
I looked at the old people. The old people looked happy.
I smiled to myself and whispered, "Thank you, Miss Muggles!"
The End…..

Printed by
EDWARDS BROTHERS
www.edwardsbrothers.com
06SKC10MDJa